At the Library

Written by Christine Loomis
Illustrated by Nancy Poydar

SCHOLASTIC INC.
NEW YORK TORONTO LONDON AUCKLAND SYDNEY

Loomis, Christine, December 1993
At the Library / by Christine Loomis; illustrated by Nancy Poydar.
p.c.m. — (Scholastic My First Library)
Summary: Rhyming text and pictures reveal a wide range of
activities being enjoyed at the local library.
ISBN 0-590-49489-9
1. Libraries — Fiction. 2. Stories in rhyme. I. Poydar, Nancy, ill. II. Title
PZ8.3.L8619Au   1994
[E] — dc20   93-10882
CIP   AC

12 11 10 9 8 7 6 5 4   7 8/9

Printed in the U.S.A.
First Scholastic printing, December 1993.

To Marcia Hupp —
librarian and friend.

— C.L.

To Ann A. Flowers in recognition of her ongoing contributions
to the field of children's literature, and with special appreciation
for her long tenure in the Children's Room.

— N.P.

At the library . . .

Open door.
Books galore!

Science, poems,
Tales of gnomes.

Kids race.
Empty space!

Prowl, peer.
Not here.

Computer tracks,
Checks stacks.

Second look.
Find book!

Grandma teaches.
Someone reaches.

Books tumble.
Big jumble!

Shelvers stack.
Books back.

Jackets on.
Baby gone!

Grandma calls.

Block falls.

Here? Where?
Check there.

Under, maybe.
No baby!

Story time.
Let's rhyme!

Out loud.
Crowd wowed!

Hands clap.
Toes tap.

Story ends.
New friends.

Shelves full.
Hands pull.

Choose two.

Check through.

Due date.
Don't be late!

No fee.
It's free . . .

At the library.